Charley Chatty
and the Wiggly Worry Worm

Charley Chatty
and the Wiggly Worry Worm

Sarah Naish and Rosie Jefferies
Illustrated by Amy Farrell

Jessica Kingsley Publishers
London and Philadelphia

First published in 2017
by Jessica Kingsley Publishers
73 Collier Street
London N1 9BE, UK
and
400 Market Street, Suite 400
Philadelphia, PA 19106, USA

www.jkp.com

Library of Congress Cataloging in Publication Data
A CIP catalog record for this book is available from the Library of Congress

British Library Cataloguing in Publication Data
A CIP catalogue record for this book is available from the British Library

ISBN 978 1 78592 149 0
eISBN 978 1 78450 410 6

Printed and bound in China

Meet Charley Chatty and her family

Charley Chatty lives with her mum, dad, brother, William Wobbly, and sisters, Rosie Rudey and Sophie Spikey. The children did not have an easy start in life and now live with their new mum and dad. All the stories are true stories. The children are real children who had difficult times, and were left feeling as if they could not trust grown-ups to sort anything out, or look after them properly. Sometimes the children were sad, sometimes very angry. Often they did things which upset other people but they did not understand why.

In this story, Charley is chatting and chatting! She knows that the more she chats, the quieter the Wiggly Worry Worm in her tummy will be. The problem is, Mum's ears are full up so she can't listen. Charley's chatting suddenly turns into a big nonsense story. Everything starts getting very mixed up and, even worse, the Wiggly Worry Worm starts moving about. Luckily, Charley's new mum is good at sorting out real stories from mixed up ones. She can even sort out the Wiggly Worry Worm. Written by Charley's mum and big sister Rosie (who is a grown-up now), this story will help everyone feel a bit better.

Charley Chatty liked to chat. She chatted and chatted and CHATTED.

Charley always chatted a lot, but she chatted even more since she had come to live with her new mum and dad.

Her brother William walked away quickly when she chatted too much. Her sister Sophie put her hands over her ears.

Her sister Rosie sighed and huffed and rudely said, "Shut up!"

She chatted so much that sometimes her mouth felt all dry, but she still kept chatting, just to make sure her mum knew that she was still there.

"Why is the pavement brown? I have got two shoes. Everyone has two shoes. I can hear the radio. Who is on the radio? Why is there a button on the radio?"

On and on the chatting went. It just wouldn't stop.

Sometimes Charley tried to stop chatting a little bit. Sometimes her dad looked at the sky a lot and made sighing noises.

When Charley stopped chatting, she felt something move inside. It was the Wiggly Worry Worm. Charley had found that chatting away, about anything at all, made the Wiggly Worry Worm keep still for a while.

One day after school, Charley was chatting away as usual, when her mum got a sighing face and said, "Sorry Charley, but my ears are too full up to hear the noisy words, they only have space left for 'important words' today."

Charley looked at the floor. She felt the Wiggly Worry Worm start to move about in her tummy. Charley tried to think really hard of some 'important words' to make her mum remember her again.

Suddenly her mouth was saying, "A man came in the woods and tried to grab Matthew!"

Mum's face went all stretchy and wide. She looked at Charley, and Charley felt the Wiggly Worry Worm calm down a bit.

Mum said, "That sounds very serious. Tell me all about it."

Charley's mouth went on and on, telling the most amazing story. All about how she had been playing in the woods with her friend Matthew. She said a man had tried to take Matthew, but she had managed to kick the man in the head and he had run away!

Mum listened carefully to Charley. Some lines appeared on her forehead. The thinking lines. Mum said, "This all sounds very worrying. Let's act it out so you can show me exactly how it happened."

Charley felt VERY important.

First she acted out playing in the woods with Matthew. She even had a few words to use up about the game they were playing.

Then they got to the bit of the story where Charley saved Matthew's life. Mum pretended to be the man. Charley was herself. Charley tried to act out kicking the man in the head but she nearly fell over as she had to make the kicks go so high.

Mum asked if the man was as tall as Charley. Charley looked at the floor and tried to remember. She couldn't remember how tall the man was. She couldn't make her leg kick high enough to reach a grown-up's head, however hard she tried.

The Wiggly Worry Worm started to move again. Charley looked at the floor. She couldn't remember the story properly and her head felt all hot and muddly.

Mum took hold of Charley's hand and said, "I think I know what happened. I think a worry worm has taken a very small story and made it much bigger. I think it started to be in charge because I said my ears were too full up of noisy talk."

Charley's hand felt a bit sweaty and hot in Mum's hand but she left it there while she tried to make some 'emergency words' come out of her mouth.

Mum said, "Let's start again with the bit where you were playing with Matthew."

Charley told the story again, but this time the man didn't come in the woods. She said, "A man walked past the woods and I THOUGHT he was going to come in."

Mum said, "It looks like that made you feel very scared, and then a worry worm took that scared feeling and made it into a scary story."

"Yes!" Charley said. "That is EXACTLY what happened!"

Charley thought her new mum must be magic. "She knows EVERYTHING!" thought Charley.

Mum said, "Sometimes, children who have had a lot of scary things happen when they were very small have worry worms left over, which can make them feel busy and fluttery inside. Don't worry though, we are stronger than this silly worm and together we can make it go away."

Charley felt very smiley at the thought that her mum was stronger than the Wiggly Worry Worm. Mum also told her that they couldn't make it go straight away, but that it would get smaller and smaller until she couldn't really feel it any more.

Later that evening, Charley went to bed. Normally, she didn't like going to bed because the Wiggly Worry Worm moved about A LOT.

Tonight, though, it seemed very quiet, Charley thought.

In fact, she couldn't feel it at all.

The End

A note for parents and carers, from the authors

This book was written to help you to help your child. All the children in the stories are based on real children and life events.

Charley Chatty has many of the behavioural and emotional issues experienced by children who have suffered developmental trauma and therefore has attachment difficulties as well as foetal alcohol spectrum disorder. You will see in this book that Charley uses 'nonsense chatter' to remind everyone she is there. You will notice how Charley becomes anxious when she cannot use 'nonsense chatter' to keep herself at the centre of her mum's world. The Wiggly Worry Worm is the manifestation of her anxiety. When Charley becomes frightened she makes up stories to help herself feel important and to make sure she is acknowledged. It is often difficult for adults around her to separate out fact from fiction.

We provide training to parents, adopters and foster carers, who have said to us that they often feel out of their depth, and do not know what to say or do when faced with these issues. This story not only gives you valuable insight into *why* our children behave this way, but also enables you to read helpful words, through the therapeutic parent (Charley's adoptive mum), to your own child.

This story not only names feelings for the child, but also gives parents and carers therapeutic parenting strategies within the story. The parent also names physical feelings. She explains to Charley why she has made up a story, and the anxiety behind it. It features some techniques which you can try in your own family:

- **Minimising 'nonsense chatter'** – The parent gives a clear indication to Charley that she is aware of her 'nonsense chatter' and that she can no longer hear it. In this way, the therapeutic parent begins to make the child more aware of their own actions and the impact it has on others. If Charley had not started to tell an alarming story, the parent may have asked her to go and write all her words down instead.

- **Acting out the story** – The parent encourages the child to re-enact the story. This helps the child to try to make sense of what she thinks has happened. Often, our children confuse facts when they are in a fear state.

- **Using touch to 'regulate'** – Many of our children function at a much younger emotional age, and never learned to control their emotions (self-regulate) as young babies. When our children are very upset, angry or spiralling out of control, simply placing a calm hand on their shoulder can help them to calm and to self-regulate. This kind of touch is not expected to be reciprocated. 'Mum' touches Charley to connect and regulate.

- **'Naming the need'** – The parent clearly names the anxiety as the 'worry worm' and speculates that it was this anxiety which has led to the story telling and exaggerating. She then relates the source of the anxiety back further to Charley's early life, to enable her to make sense of her own behaviours and reactions.

- **Being the 'secure base'** – Charley's mum states very clearly that she knows what is happening and that she is stronger than the 'worry worm'.

Sarah is a therapeutic parent of five adopted siblings, now all adults, former social worker and owner of an 'Outstanding' therapeutic fostering agency. Rosie is her daughter, and checked and amended Charley's thoughts and expressed feelings to ensure they are as accurate a reflection as possible. Together, we now spend all our time training and helping parents, carers, social workers and other professionals to heal traumatised children.

Please use this story to make connections, explain behaviours, and build attachments between your child and yourself.

Therapeutic parenting makes everything possible.

Warmest regards,

Sarah Naish and Rosie Jefferies

If you liked Charley Chatty, why not meet Callum Kindly, Katie Careful, William Wobbly, Sophie Spikey and Rosie Rudey

---

William Wobbly and the Mysterious Holey Jumper

A story about fear and coping

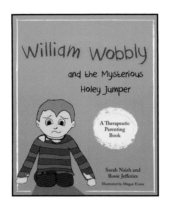

Callum Kindly and the Very Weird Child

A story about sharing your home with a new child

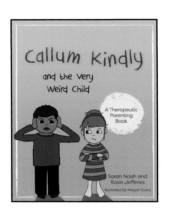

Rosie Rudey and the Very Annoying Parent

A story about a prickly child who is scared of getting close

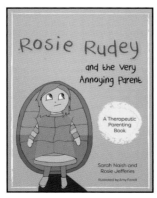

Katie Careful and the Very Sad Smile

A story about anxious and clingy behaviour

Sophie Spikey Has a Very Big Problem

A story about refusing help and needing to be in control

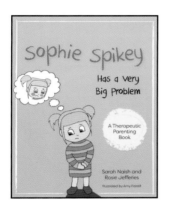

William Wobbly and the Very Bad Day

A story about when feelings become too big

Rosie Rudey and the Enormous Chocolate Mountain

A story about hunger, overeating and using food for comfort

Charley Chatty and the Disappearing Pennies

A story about lying and stealing